LOUISIANA 1800

MISSISSIPPI RIVER

GULF OF MEXICO

OLD *Hasdrubal*
AND THE
Pirates

By Berthe Amoss

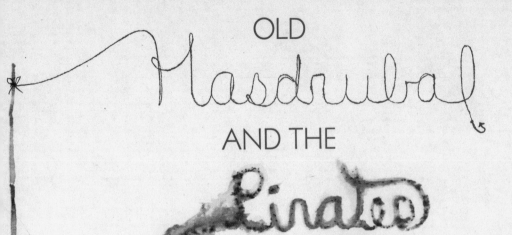

PARENTS' MAGAZINE PRESS/NEW YORK

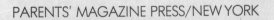

Back in bayou Barataria, Billy and Old Hannibal
were fishing for catfish.

Old Hannibal opened one eye, swatted a mosquito,
and watched a white heron disappear into the swamp.
"Pirate country, Billy boy," he said, nodding in the

direction the bird had flown. "Lafitte's old lair."

"Jean Lafitte? He was a famous pirate, wasn't he, Old Hannibal?" asked Billy, baiting his hook.

"A famous pirate! Billy boy, he was the MOST
famous pirate. Handsome, bold, fearless and peer-
less, he and his men sailed the seas, capturing
ships of every nation—galleons full of silver and
gold, precious gems and diadems, diamond tiaras
and lace madeiras, festooned dragoons and doubloons
from tycoons! Then, in their pirogues, Lafitte and
his men slipped back to hideouts in the labyrinth
swamp where no man could seek them out."
Old Hannibal paused and threw out a line. "No man,
that is, except . . .

"Old great-great-grandfather Hasdrubal!"

"*Your* great-great-grandfather, Old Hannibal?
Did he find Lafitte, himself?" asked Billy,
watching his cork.
"That he did," said Old Hannibal, "*and* was the
unsung hero of the Battle of New Orleans—back
in 1815."
"Tell me about it, Old Hannibal. Please!"
"Well, it happened like this, Billy boy," said
Old Hannibal, easing back against the gunnel.

"One day Old great-great-grandfather Hasdrubal
was fishing in the bayou. He was getting sleepy
listening to the hum of insects.

Suddenly, his cork went under with the force of
a bullet. A great tail slashed the water!

Old great-great-grandfather Hasdrubal had hooked
an alligator and was fighting—or, you might say,
fishing—for his life!

At times, it looked bad for Old great-great-grandfather Hasdrubal.

But, finally, he lassoed those gaping jaws, and
soon after, Mr. Alligator parted with his skin.

Now Old great-great-grandfather Hasdrubal was
about to shove off, when he heard the sound of
paddled pirogues in the sultry swamp. He pushed
his pirogue into high marsh grasses just before
a dozen pirates with a captive maid glided into
sight and landed on a shell bank.

They bound the lovely girl to a tree and hoisted
a chest ponderous with plunder onto the land. As they
mapped and buried the treasure, Old great-great-

grandfather Hasdrubal thought quick. He slipped into that alligator skin, slithered into the slimy swamp, and sneaked up behind the pirates.

He opened wide his 'gator jaws and said, 'Ah! Ah! AH!'

There never was a quicker exit in the history of the world! Those buccaneers bucked out of there with the speed of sound, leaving treasure, map, and girl. Old great-great-grandfather Hasdrubal didn't wait to change his outfit. He stuffed the map into his alligator skin, cut the ropes that bound the maid, and threw her over his shoulder— she having fainted with fright. He leaped into his pirogue and paddled for home.

Meanwhile, the pirates reported to their
Captain Lafitte.
'Alligators don't say Ah, Ah, Ah!' bellowed
Lafitte. 'It's a trick, you nincompoops!
Heave Ho, me Hearties, and after them!'

At his command, two thousand fierce pirates shoved their pirogues into the swamp in pursuit of Old great-great-grandfather Hasdrubal and the fair maid. They tracked them through the winding waterways to the outskirts of New Orleans. At that very moment, the brave but outnumbered Americans were fighting to save the city from the British Redcoats.

Suddenly, the startled Redcoats saw an alligator running on his hind legs and carrying a dazed but dazzling damsel in distress.

'Zounds and zoots!' exclaimed the British commander. 'What a country!'

He was about to give the order to advance,
when out of the woods dashed the screaming pirates,
knives in teeth, cutlasses brandished.

'Leave the land to the loonies!' cried the British commander.
No Redcoat lingered long to look. They ran to
their frigates and sailed within the hour.

Lafitte and the pirates were hailed as heroes
in New Orleans.

And Old great-great-grandfather Hasdrubal—having shed his unnatural skin—was a hero to the maid.

'Just like the frog prince,' she sighed, and shortly after became Old great-great-grandmother Hasdrubal.

"And that, Billy boy, no matter what you may read to the contrary, is how and why Lafitte and the pirates turned patriots and saved the city!"

"But the treasure, Old Hannibal, what became of the treasure? Did Old great-great-grandfather Hasdrubal go back and find it? And did you get any of it?"

"One question at a time, Billy boy, one question at a time! It happened like this.

"You see, Old great-great-grandfather Hasdrubal. intended going back, of course, but—he was prevented by a culinary disaster!"

"A what, Old Hannibal?" asked Billy. "*How* was he prevented?"

"Well, Billy, one day shortly after Old great-great-grandfather Hasdrubal and Old great-great-grandmother were married, Old great-great-grandmother Hasdrubal was attempting to cook gumbo for dinner.

She was reading the recipe she had gotten from her
mother-in-law and unwittingly scribbled on the back
of the treasure map. Just as she was about to stir
in the filé—a vital and powdery ingredient—

she SNEEZED

and blew the recipe-map into the pot! It was quickly blended into the gumbo, making a richer dish but a poorer family!

"Well, Billy?"

"What a line, Old Hannibal," said Billy, laughing. "I mean, *watch* your line. You have a catfish, and we have dinner!"

A Note from the Author

Old great-great-grandfather Hasdrubal is not mentioned
in Billy's history book. Lafitte is. He did, unaccountably
and temporarily, change from pirate to patriot,
and he was the hero (along with Andrew Jackson)
of the Battle of New Orleans (1815) during the
War of 1812.
There *was* treasure buried in Barataria, the swampland
Lafitte and his pirates inhabited, and fortune hunters
still search for it. But the pirate gold lies hidden
in the past, as much a mystery as Lafitte himself.

NEW ORLEANS
BATTLE OF NEW ORLEANS
BAYOU BARATARIA
SWAMP
BARATARIA BAY